Sweet Pea & Friends

A Farm for Maisie

By John and Jennifer Churchman

LITTLE, BROWN AND COMPANY
NEW YORK   BOSTON

Maisie Grace looked out at the swirling snow.
Today she would be going to her new home,
a farm and family of her very own.

At Moonrise Farm, all the animals were so excited to meet the new puppy. Sweet Pea stuck her head out the barn window. "She's here! I can see her!" she cried joyfully.

Farmer John introduced little Maisie, and Laddie greeted the black-and-white puppy with a curious sniff. "Laddie," Farmer John said, "you will be responsible for showing her around the farm."

Laddie felt proud that the farmer trusted him so much.

Maisie cautiously reached out and touched Sweet Pea's nose. She had never met a sheep before.

"We're so happy you are here," Sweet Pea said with a smile. Maisie was glad to have a new friend.

Cyrie and Quinn, the farmhouse dogs, suggested Maisie come on their morning run.

"Call to Laddie if you can't keep up," Sweet Pea told her as the dogs took off for the woods.

"I can do it!" barked Maisie.

Maisie ran as fast as her little legs would go, but she could not keep up with Laddie and the older dogs.

She soon grew tired.
Her paws were wet and
cold. She sat on the side of
the trail, her lip trembling.
She wanted to go everywhere
the big dogs went.

Then she saw Laddie bounding through the snow. He was coming back for her! Maisie breathed a sigh of relief. "Don't worry," said Laddie. "I'll ask Farmer John to give you a ride."

Farmer John picked up Maisie and held her close. "Would you like to help with farm chores, little one?" Maisie felt much better.

"Everyone on the farm has a special job," Laddie explained. First, they would visit the paddock to feed Sadie the pony.

"What is Sadie's job?" Maisie asked.

"Sadie pulls supplies in her pony cart
from here to there and back again,
helping Farmer John," said Laddie.

Maisie wasn't sure she could pull a cart,
but she wanted to have a job, too.

Next, they stopped to feed the sheep. Maisie saw her new friend Sweet Pea standing nearby, smiling. "Do the sheep have jobs on the farm?" Maisie asked Laddie.

"Of course!" he said. "Sweet Pea and all the sheep keep the farm fields healthy by eating the grass. And they have soft wool, which is spun into beautiful yarn to make blankets, hats, mittens, sweaters, and even toys."

Being able to make warm and wonderful things sounded magical to Maisie. She wanted to do something just as special.

Next, they headed to the henhouse to feed grain to the chickens, ducks, and turkeys.

"They all lay eggs," said Laddie. "Some eggs are sold at the market, and some are used in the farmhouse for cooking."

Maisie was *sure* she could not lay an egg!
As she admired all the pretty colors, she
wondered what she *would* be able to do.

What was all that noise?!
Maisie saw the geese flapping
their wings and honking loudly.
They were making quite a racket.
What was going on?

"The geese guard the chickens, ducks, and turkeys from the forest fox who likes to eat their eggs," said Laddie.

"Oh!" said Maisie seriously. That sounded like a very important job. She liked the idea of guarding and protecting. Maybe she could help the geese?

It was almost time for dinner. With all the chores done, Maisie and Laddie headed back to the farmhouse. While Farmer Jennifer gave her a bath, Maisie was lost in thought. What would her farm job be?

As she and little Finn the lamb nibbled their dinner in the warm farmhouse kitchen, she wondered some more.

As she settled by the fireplace, Maisie thought back on her day. *The sheep have wool for yarn and keep the pastures beautiful,* she remembered. *The chicken, ducks, and turkeys lay eggs, and the geese protect them from the fox. Sadie the pony pulls the cart....I can't do any of those things!*

Maisie began to worry. This was her new home, and she wanted to belong. "Laddie," she asked shyly, "will I have a job someday?"

"Oh yes," Laddie said kindly. "We are *sheepdogs*, Maisie— soon you will have one of the most important jobs of all."

As winter turned to spring, Maisie watched how Laddie took care of the sheep. He herded them to the pastures in the morning and brought them back to the warm barn at night. He helped Farmer John separate them into pens for shearing, hoof clipping, and checkups.

Laddie made sure the sheep were always safe and let Farmer John know if something was wrong.

He took his job of guiding and protecting his flock very seriously, and he was a wonderful teacher to Maisie.

The more Maisie learned about being a sheepdog, the more she *loved* it.

While in the barn late one afternoon, Maisie heard a strange sound. Her ears perked up, and the tip of her tail began to tingle....

It sounded like a lamb crying!

Maisie found the youngest lamb, Atticus, with his hoof stuck in the hay feeder. He was alone and scared. "Don't worry, Atticus—I'll get help!" she reassured him, and ran as fast as she could to get Farmer John.

Farmer John gently lifted Atticus from the feeder. "Well done, Maisie!" he said. "I think you are ready for a flock of your own."

A flock of my own! Maisie beamed.

Over the spring, Maisie started
to care for her four little lambs,
Atticus, Hayzel, Meadow, and
Finn, all by herself.

She loved being a sheepdog.
To her, it was the best job of all.

Each night, as Maisie snuggled into bed, she felt thankful. She had a farm and a family, new friends, and an important job of her very own.

She fell asleep happily, dreaming of her little lambs and counting them—one, two, three ...

The True Story of Maisie Grace

From the moment Maisie Grace arrived at Moonrise Farm, her sweet and earnest personality won over everyone she encountered. As a pup, she would follow Laddie and John around, and light up at the sight of the lambs and sheep. You could just see her tingling with anticipation to help, waiting for the day she'd have her own job minding them. To a border collie like Maisie, working on a sheep farm is a dream come true. Nothing makes her happier than doing chores around the farm and watching over her charges. In the winter, when it's too cold for the sheep to graze, she and Laddie still keep their minds and paws busy. This year, we will be training them to pull a dogsled as a team.

Maisie Grace was named after her maternal grandmother, Grace. We love the way her name sounds when we call out to her as she joyfully runs across the farm fields: just like "Amazing Grace." And that, she certainly is.

Life at Moonrise Farm

The portrayal of every job in the story is a true reflection of how each animal helps us run a successful and fulfilling operation. Maisie and Laddie help with the sheep, of course, and Sadie and the sheep, chickens, ducks, and geese contribute in their own way. Even our honeybees play a role, pollinating our plants and providing us with honey. We, in turn, keep our kitchen garden right outside their hive door for them to enjoy.

Behind the Scenes: Storytelling Inspiration

I've been a storyteller all my life. I spent my childhood writing, and reading *Charlotte's Web, Winnie-the-Pooh, The Velveteen Rabbit,* and the works of Beatrix Potter—stories where the animals talked to one another were my favorites. Growing up on a small sheep farm, I was always surrounded by animals. An observer by nature, I often found myself with thoughts like, *What are those chickens always talking about, anyway?* I have my family to thank for

Farmer John and Maisie feeding the flock

Laddie, Quinn, and Cyrie

Moonrise Farm chickens

Maisie napping with a friend

that. My mother drew my attention to all the details of everyday life, from the patterns in the clouds to how the seasons change the look of the landscape. She taught me that the natural world has more than meets the eye. My brother, Michael, sister, Gillian, and I would tell stories to one another, making treasure maps and creating elaborate adventures in the woods and farmland that surrounded our home. We were lucky to be raised in an environment where imagination and creativity were highly valued, and we were given lots of time for both. One of my favorite childhood memories is coming upon my father having a conversation with his beloved border collie, Tip. I was fascinated to realize that they could communicate with each other in their own individual languages. I have never looked at animals the same way since.

Our Sweet Pea & Friends series is a collaborative effort, where words meet art to tell a story, bringing our farm to life in a new way. First, John and I take photos, capturing the narratives that unfold by observing our animals in their natural environments. Once we've come to a story, we sketch a storyboard. I write the first draft of the text, and John arranges layer upon layer of photographs, blending them digitally as he would layer paint on a canvas by hand, a technique he calls fine-art photo-illustration. We combine text and art, each gently nudging here and there, meeting somewhere in the middle and letting the book take on a life of its own. And so the storytelling tradition continues.

—Jennifer

Special Thanks

This book was created with the support and encouragement of friends, family, and followers of Maisie's story online. We would like to thank our agent, Brenda Bowen; editors, Megan Tingley and Allison Moore; and the whole team at Little, Brown Books for Young Readers. We'd also like to give a special thanks to all the booksellers in the Vermont area and beyond who have championed our books.

The story doesn't end here! Join the animals for more adventures at sweetpeafriends.com.

Storyboard sketchbook

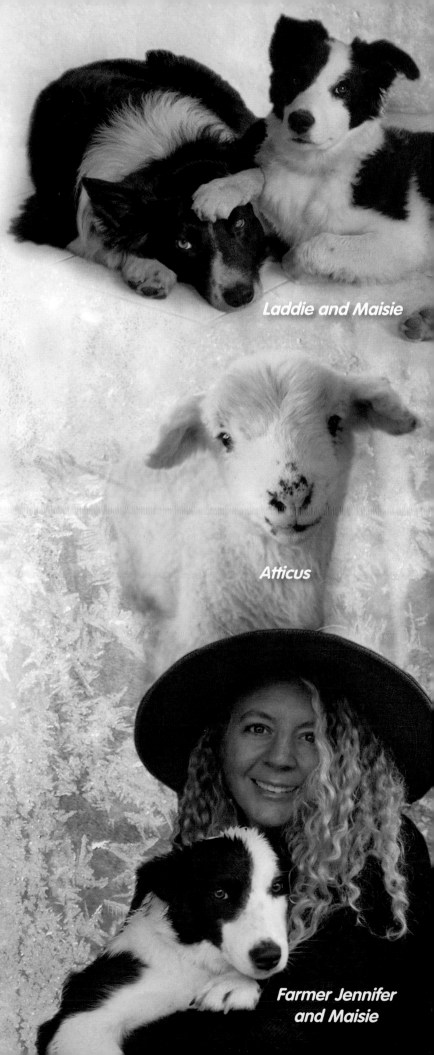

Laddie and Maisie

Atticus

Farmer Jennifer and Maisie

Dedicated with love to our children,
Kailie, Travis, and Gabrielle.
And to our parents,
Patricia and Charles Churchman
and Richard and Kate Flies,
for always believing in us.

Little, Brown and Company
Hachette Book Group
1290 Avenue of the Americas, New York, NY 10104
Visit us at lb-kids.com

First Edition: October 2017

Little, Brown and Company is a division of Hachette Book Group, Inc.
The Little, Brown name and logo are trademarks of Hachette Book Group, Inc.

The publisher is not responsible for websites (or their
content) that are not owned by the publisher.

ISBNs: 978-0-316-27360-2 (hardcover)
978-0-316-27364-0 (ebook)
978-0-316-50689-2 (ebook)
978-0-316-50688-5 (ebook)

Printed in China

1010

10 9 8 7 6 5 4 3 2 1